The Summoning of Everyman: A Medieval Morality Play (A Retelling)

David Bruce

Published by David Bruce, 2023.

THE SUMMONING OF EVERYMAN: A MEDIEVAL MORALITY PLAY (A RETELLING)

First edition. January 30, 2023.

Copyright © 2023 David Bruce.

ISBN: 979-8215385654

Written by David Bruce.

Table of Contents

CAST OF CHARACTERS 1

PROLOGUE 3

CHAPTER 1 5

CHAPTER 2 16

CHAPTER 3 27

CHAPTER 4 36

CHAPTER 5 42

EPILOGUE 47

NOTES 48

PETER SINGER: THE ARGUMENT TO ASSIST 57

BIBLE VERSES ABOUT GOOD DEEDS 62

APPENDIX A: FAIR USE 64

APPENDIX B: ABOUT THE AUTHOR 65

APPENDIX C: SOME BOOKS BY DAVID BRUCE 66

Dedication

Dedicated to Carl Eugene Bruce and Josephine Saturday Bruce

My father, Carl Eugene Bruce, died on 24 October 2013. He used to work for Ohio Power, and at one time, his job was to shut off the electricity of people who had not paid their bills. He sometimes would find a home with an impoverished mother and some children. Instead of shutting off their electricity, he would tell the mother that she needed to pay her bill or soon her electricity would be shut off. He would write on a form that no one was home when he stopped by because if no one was home he did not have to shut off their electricity.

The best good deed that anyone ever did for my father occurred after a storm that knocked down many power lines. He and other linemen worked long hours and got wet and cold. Their feet were freezing because water got into their boots and soaked their socks. Fortunately, a kind woman gave my father and the other linemen dry socks to wear.

My mother, Josephine Saturday Bruce, died on 14 June 2003. She used to work at a store that sold clothing. One day, an impoverished mother with a baby clothed in rags walked into the store and started shoplifting in an interesting way: The mother took the rags off her baby and dressed the infant in new clothing. My mother knew that this mother could not afford to buy the clothing, but she helped the mother dress her baby and then she watched as the mother walked out of the store without paying.

***

The doing of good deeds is important. As a free person, you can choose to live your life as a good person or as a bad person. To be a good person, do good deeds. To be a bad person, do bad deeds. If you do good deeds, you will become good. If you do bad deeds, you will become bad. To become the person you want to be, act as if you already are that kind of person. Each of us chooses what kind of person we will become. To become a good person, do the things a good person does. To become a bad person, do the things a bad person does. The opportunity to take action to become the kind of person you want to be is yours.

Human beings have free will. According to the Babylonian Niddah 16b, whenever a baby is to be conceived, the Lailah (angel in charge of contraception) takes the drop of semen that will result in the conception and asks God, "Sovereign of the Universe, what is going to be the fate of this drop? Will it develop into a robust or into a weak person? An intelligent or a stupid person? A wealthy or a poor person?" The Lailah asks all these questions, but it does not ask, "Will it develop into a righteous or a wicked person?" The answer to that question lies in the decisions to be freely made by the human being that is the result of the conception.

A Buddhist monk visiting a class wrote this on the chalkboard: "EVERYONE WANTS TO SAVE THE WORLD, BUT NO ONE WANTS TO HELP MOM DO THE DISHES." The students laughed, but the monk then said, "Statistically, it's highly unlikely that any of you will ever have the opportunity to run into a burning orphanage and rescue an infant. But, in the smallest gesture of kindness — a warm smile, holding the door for the person behind you, shoveling the driveway of the elderly person next door — you have committed an act of immeasurable profundity, because to each of us, our life is our universe."

Cover Photo for *The Summoning of Everyman*: A Medieval Morality Play (A Retelling):

Open Clipart-Vectors

https://pixabay.com/vectors/skull-day-of-the-dead-2028286/

Educate Yourself
Read Like A Wolf Eats
Be Excellent to Each Other
Books Then, Books Now, Books Forever

***

In this retelling, as in all my retellings, I have tried to make the work of literature accessible to modern readers who may lack some of the knowledge about mythology, religion, and history that the literary work's contemporary audience had.

Do you know a language other than English? If you do, I give you permission to translate this book, copyright your translation, publish or self-publish it, and keep all the royalties for yourself. (Do give me credit, of course, for the original retelling.)

I would like to see my retellings of classic literature used in schools, so I give permission to the country of Finland (and all other countries) to give copies of any or all of my retellings to all students forever. I also give permission to the state of Texas (and all other states) to give copies of any or all of my retellings to all students forever. I also give permission to all teachers to give copies of any or all of my retellings to all students forever. Of course, libraries are welcome to use my eBooks for free.

Teachers need not actually teach my retellings. Teachers are welcome to give students copies of my eBooks as background material. For example, if they are teaching Homer's *Iliad* and *Odyssey*, teachers are welcome to give students copies of my *Virgil's Aeneid: A Retelling in Prose* and tell students, "Here's another ancient epic you may want to read in your spare time."

Dedicated to Carl Eugene Bruce and Josephine Saturday Bruce

My father, Carl Eugene Bruce, died on 24 October 2013. He used to work for Ohio Power, and at one time, his job was to shut off the electricity of people who had not paid their bills. He sometimes would find a home with an impoverished mother and some children. Instead of shutting off their electricity, he would tell the mother that she needed to pay her bill or soon her electricity would be shut off. He would write on a form that no one was home when he stopped by because if no one was home he did not have to shut off their electricity.

The best good deed that anyone ever did for my father occurred after a storm that knocked down many power lines. He and other linemen worked long hours and got wet and cold. Their feet were freezing because water got into their boots and soaked their socks. Fortunately, a kind woman gave my father and the other linemen dry socks to wear.

My mother, Josephine Saturday Bruce, died on 14 June 2003. She used to work at a store that sold clothing. One day, an impoverished mother with a baby clothed in rags walked into the store and started shoplifting in an interesting way: The mother took the rags off her baby and dressed the infant in new clothing. My mother knew that this mother could not afford to buy the clothing, but she helped the mother dress her baby and then she watched as the mother walked out of the store without paying.

***

The doing of good deeds is important. As a free person, you can choose to live your life as a good person or as a bad person. To be a good person, do good deeds. To be a bad person, do bad deeds. If you do good deeds, you will become good. If you do bad deeds, you will become bad. To become the person you want to be, act as if you already are that kind of person. Each of us chooses what kind of person we will become. To become a good person, do the things a good person does. To become a bad person, do the things a bad person does. The opportunity to take action to become the kind of person you want to be is yours.

Human beings have free will. According to the Babylonian Niddah 16b, whenever a baby is to be conceived, the Lailah (angel in charge of contraception) takes the drop of semen that will result in the conception and asks God, "Sovereign of the Universe, what is going to be the fate of this drop? Will it develop into a robust or into a weak person? An intelligent or a stupid person? A wealthy or a poor person?" The Lailah asks all these questions, but it does not ask, "Will it develop into a righteous or a wicked person?" The answer to that question lies in the decisions to be freely made by the human being that is the result of the conception.

A Buddhist monk visiting a class wrote this on the chalkboard: "EVERYONE WANTS TO SAVE THE WORLD, BUT NO ONE WANTS TO HELP MOM DO THE DISHES." The students laughed, but the monk then said, "Statistically, it's highly unlikely that any of you will ever have the opportunity to run into a burning orphanage and rescue an infant. But, in the smallest gesture of kindness — a warm smile, holding the door for the person behind you, shoveling the driveway of the elderly person next door — you have committed an act of immeasurable profundity, because to each of us, our life is our universe."

CAST OF CHARACTERS

Everyman.

***

Messenger.
　God.
　Death.

***

Fellowship.
　Kindred.
　Cousin.
　Goods.

***

Good Deeds.
　Knowledge.
　Confession.
　Beauty.
　Strength.
　Discretion.
　Five Wits.

***

Angel.
　Doctor of Theology.
　NOTES:
"Everyman" means "every person, male or female."

When reading this book, you may want to mentally substitute [Your Name] for Everyman.

The Middle Ages occurred before the Protestant Reformation, so all Christians are Catholic or Eastern Orthodox. In this book, they are Catholic.

This play is Christian, and so it contains Christian theology.

The word "Goods" means "Wealth."

Everyman must die and must give an account of his life and deeds to God. He must do this without delay, so after Death comes to him, he will have no time remaining to amend his life. His account will include his sins and his good deeds. This account of his life is called a reckoning.

When you die, your wealth immediately leaves you. Your family and best friends will accompany you to your grave. (In this book, Everyman's family and best friends don't even do that.) Only your Good Deeds will go with you to plead your case before God on the Judgment Day.

The Five Wits are memory, fantasy, judgment (aka estimation), imagination, and common sense. These are the five inward wits.

But possibly, the Five Wits are the five outward wits: the five senses, which are seeing, hearing, touching, tasting, and smelling.

In this society, a person of higher rank would use "thou," "thee," "thine," and "thy" when referring to a person of lower rank. (These terms were also used affectionately and between equals.) A person of lower rank would use "you" and "your" when referring to a person of higher rank.

PROLOGUE

Here begins a story about how the High Father of Heaven sends Death to summon every creature to come and give an account of his or her life and deeds in this world; this story is in the form of a moral play.

A Messenger appeared. Divine messengers do such things as tell Mary that she will give birth to the Son of God.

The Messenger said to you, the audience:

"I ask all of you to pay attention and hear and read this matter with reverence and respect.

"In form this is a moral play. It is called *The Summoning of Everyman*, which of our lives and their ending in death shows how transitory and temporary we always are.

"The theme of the play is wondrously precious and of great moral value, but its intention and purpose is more gracious and devout, and sweet to remember and bear away."

The theme of the play is death, and its purpose is to inform the reader how to prepare him- or herself for the Last Judgment, in which God will decide who will go to Hell and who will go to Heaven.

The Messenger continued:

"The story says:

"Humankind, listen: In the beginning look well, and take good heed to the ending."

In other words: Pay attention to how you lead your life, and no matter how happy you are now, be always aware that how you lead your life will determine where you end up in the afterlife.

The Messenger continued:

"You think that in the beginning sin is very sweet, but in the end, sin causes thy soul to weep, when the body lies buried in clay.

"Here you shall see how Fellowship and Jollity, and how Strength, Pleasure, and Beauty will fade from thee as flowers fade in May, for you shall hear how our Heavenly King calls Everyman to a general account and reckoning of his conduct in his life.

"Pay attention, and hear what our Heavenly King says."

The Messenger exited.

CHAPTER 1

Summary: Everyman learns that he will die soon and that he must account for his life and deeds.

On the stage, Goods and Good Deeds were near each other. Goods sat among evidence of material wealth such as money bags. Good Deeds lay, weak and unable to stand, near Everyman's book of account.

A book of account records all deeds and motives of a person's life.

God entered the scene. He was in the balcony above the stage.

God said:

"I perceive here in My Majesty that all creatures — all humans — are to me unkind, ungrateful, and unnatural, living without dread in worldly, material prosperity:

"When it comes to spiritual vision, the people are so blind. Drowned in sin, they don't know me, their God.

"All their mind is focused on worldly riches. They don't fear my righteousness, the sharp rod of my justice.

"They have entirely forgotten my divine law that I showed them, when I died for them, and they have forgotten the shedding of my red blood."

The Bible contains divine law: commandments that God wants people to follow.

A basic tenet of Christian theology is that Jesus died for our sins. He endured the punishment that we sinners deserve to suffer, and because of that, we sinners have the chance to repent our sins and be given the gift of eternal life.

God continued:

"I hanged between two sinners; it cannot be denied. To bring life for them and for all people, I consented to die and I suffered death."

When Jesus Christ was crucified, He was crucified in between two criminals. Jesus is part of the Trinity. God is a tripartite God: the Father, the Son, and the Holy Ghost.

Matthew 27:38 states, "*There were two thieves crucified with him, one on the right hand, and another on the left*" (King James Version).

Jesus died, and after three days, he was resurrected.

God continued:

"I healed their feet."

Jesus washed the feet of His disciples.

John 13:12-15 states (King James Version):

12 So after he had washed their feet, and had taken his garments, and was set down again, he said unto them, Know ye what I have done to you?

13 Ye call me Master and Lord: and ye say well; for so I am.

14 If I then, your Lord and Master, have washed your feet; ye also ought to wash one another's feet.

15 For I have given you an example, that ye should do as I have done to you.

God continued:

"My head was hurt with thorns."

When Jesus was crucified, he wore a crown of thorns.

Matthew 27:29 states, "*And when they had platted a crown of thorns, they put it upon his head, and a reed in his right hand: and they bowed the knee before him, and mocked him, saying, Hail, King of the Jews!*" (King James Version).

God continued:

"I could do no more than I did truly, and now I see that the people entirely forsake me: They engage in the seven damnable deadly sins, such as pride, covetousness and greed, wrath, and lechery and lust. Now in the world the seven deadly sins have been made commendable and praiseworthy."

The three other deadly sins are envy, gluttony, and sloth.

According to author Richard G. Newhauser, editor of *The Seven Deadly Sins*, these are *deadly* sins "because they lead to the death of the soul."

God continued:

"And thus human beings reject the Heavenly company of angels.

"Every man lives so entirely after his own pleasure, and yet human beings' lives are not at all secure.

"I see that the more I refrain from punishing them, the worse they become from year to year.

"All who live quickly grow worse and become corrupt.

"Therefore, I will in all haste have a reckoning of each person, for if I leave the people thus alone in their lives and wicked tempests and commotions, truly they will become much worse than beasts.

"For now because of envy one person would eat up and destroy another person.

"They all entirely forget charity.

"I hoped well that every man should make his mansion in my glory — in Heaven — and in that place I had them all chosen to reside, but now I see, like abject traitors, they don't thank me for the pleasure that I meant for them, nor yet for their existence that I have lent them."

John 14:2 states, "*In my Father's house are many mansions: if it were not so, I would have told you. I go to prepare a place for you*" (King James Version).

Life is a gift from God.

God continued:

"I proffered the people a great multitude of mercy, and few there are who ask for it heartily — with their hearts.

"Humans are so encumbered and spiritually burdened by worldly riches that I must necessarily do justice on every man living without fear of Me."

Fear of God can mean awe of and submission to God. A person who fears God will obey God's commandments. That can be done because of fear of ending up in Hell, but it can be done out of reverence and respect for God and for what is right. People can fear to do evil.

God then asked:

"Where are thou, Death, thou mighty messenger?"

Death entered the scene.

"Almighty God, I am here at your will, and I am here to fulfil Your commandment," Death said.

God said, "Go to Everyman, and show him in my name a pilgrimage — a spiritual journey — he must take on himself, which in no way he may escape. And tell him that he must bring with him a sure, trustworthy, and true reckoning — an account — of his life without delay or any tarrying."

Everyman must die and then give an account of his life to God. He must do this without delay; after Everyman dies, he will have no time remaining to amend his life. His reckoning will include an account of his sins and of his good deeds.

Death said:

"Lord, I will run throughout the entire world, and I will unrelentingly search out both great and small.

"I will beset and assail everyone who lives like a beast, out of God's laws, and who does not dread folly. I will strike with my dart everyone who loves riches, and unless alms, charity, and good deeds are his good friend, I will blind his sight, I will separate him from Heaven, and I will make him dwell in Hell, a world without end, forever.

"Look, yonder I see Everyman walking: Very little he thinks about my — Death's — coming. He does not expect me. His mind is on fleshly lusts and his treasure, and it shall cause him great pain to endure giving an account of his life before the Lord Heaven King."

Finely dressed, Everyman entered the scene.

God remained on the balcony and was silent.

Death said:

"Everyman, stand still. Where are thou going thus gaily? Have thou forgotten thy Maker?"

Everyman asked, "Why do thou ask? Would thou know the answer?"

"Yes, sir, I will show you where thou are going," Death said. "In great haste I am sent to thee by God out of his Majesty."

"What! Sent to me?" Everyman said.

Death said: "Yes, certainly I am sent to thee. Although you have forgotten Him here, He thinks about thee in the Heavenly sphere, as, before we depart, thou shall know."

The medieval conception of the cosmos was that the Earth is at the center of the universe. People believed that over the Earth are a number of crystalline spheres, one of which is a sphere of fire. Other spheres held the Sun, the Moon, various planets, and the fixed stars (they are fixed in position to each other; in contrast, the planets are not fixed in position to each other — they wander in the sky). The modern conception of the cosmos is much different; modern scientists think of the cosmos as consisting mostly of empty space and dark matter and dark energy. Medieval thinkers believed that each celestial sphere made contact with the sphere above it and with the sphere below it. The outermost sphere is the Mystic Empyrean: It is beyond space and time, and it is the dwelling place of God.

"What does God want of me?" Everyman asked.

Death said, "That I shall tell thee: A reckoning he must necessarily have, without any longer respite or further delay."

When Death comes for you, there is no time left to you to amend your life — you are dead. You must give an account of your life as you have lived it.

Sometimes, you know that Death is coming for you. You know that you will die quickly: in a minute, an hour, a day, a week, a month, or a year. In such a case, you may be able to set your affairs in order and get ready to face God. Everyman is not yet dead, but he knows that he will die soon, although he does not want to die.

Everyman said, "To give a reckoning, I crave longer leisure: This blind matter — this situation I am not prepared for — troubles my mind."

Everyman wanted to live longer so he could prepare himself to meet God.

Death said:

"Thou must undertake a long journey:

"Therefore, bring with thee thy book of the account of thy life and deeds, for thou cannot by any way return again to life."

Revelation 20:12 states, *"And I saw the dead, small and great, stand before God; and the books were opened: and another book was opened, which is the book of life: and the dead were judged out of those things which were written in the books, according to their works"* (King James Bible).

Death continued:

"And look that thou are unerring in giving an account of thy life, for before God thou shall answer and show thy many bad deeds, and thou very few good deeds.

"Thou shall say how thou have spent thy life, and in what wise, before the chief lord of Paradise: God.

"Get going and let's go on our way, for, know thou well, thou shall make no one thy attorney to speak for you."

Everyone, including Everyman, will not be able to pay anyone to speak for him or her: He or she will have to speak for him- or herself.

"I am entirely unready to give such a reckoning of my life," Everyman said. "I don't know thee. What messenger are thou?"

"I am Death, who fears no man, for every man I arrest, and I spare no man, for it is God's commandment that all to me should be obedient," Death said.

Everyman said:

"O Death, thou have come when I had thee least in mind! In thy power it lies to save me.

"Yet if thou will be kind, I will give thee some of my goods. Yes, thou shall have a thousand pounds, if thou will defer this matter until another day."

A thousand pounds in the Middle Ages was a vast amount of money. Everyman was wealthy. He attempted to bribe Death, but Death cannot be bribed.

Death said:

"Everyman, that will not happen.

"I set no value on gold, silver, or riches, nor do I set any value on the titles of pope, emperor, king, duke, and princes.

"For, if I wanted to accept great gifts, I could get all the world, but my custom is completely to the contrary.

"I give thee no respite: Come away from here, and do not tarry."

Everyman said:

"Alas! Shall I have no longer respite? I may say Death gives no warning.

"To think about thee, it makes my heart sick, for my book of reckoning is not at all ready.

"But, if I could live for twelve more years, I would make my accounting-book so clear and spotless that I would not need to fear my reckoning.

"Therefore, Death, I pray thee for God's mercy! Spare me, until I have provided myself a remedy and have reformed my life!"

Death said:

"It does not help thee to cry, weep, and pray.

"But hasten thee quickly, so that thou can be gone on that journey, and test thy friends, if thou can.

"For, as thou know well, time waits for no man, and in the world each living creature — each human being — because of Adam's sin must die in the course of nature."

Everyman is going to die very soon, and he has little time to amend his life, but Death gives him the opportunity to talk to his friends to see if any of them will accompany him on his journey to God so they can help him give an accounting of his life.

Imagine being on your deathbed, knowing that you will die soon, and wishing that you had more time to do good with your life. In such a case, Death may come immediately, but Death may come a little later, giving you an opportunity to talk with people before you die.

On your deathbed, you can amend your life. You can pray, repent, and receive the Last Rites. In Dante's *Purgatory*, people who repent at the end of their life are saved, but they must wait for a while to begin climbing the Mountain of Purgatory. They kept God waiting, and so God justly makes them wait for a while.

But on your deathbed, your ability to do good deeds and to try to amend the bad effects of your bad deeds is limited, although you may be able to make a will that does good.

The most important ethical rule is this: Do no evil. Do not do to others what you do not want done to yourself.

But since everyone sins, this ethical rule is also important: Do some good. Do to others what you want done to you.

In the Garden of Eden, Adam committed the original sin. Because of that, human beings must die.

Genesis 3:19 states, "*In the sweat of thy face shalt thou eat bread, till thou return unto the ground; for out of it wast thou taken: for dust thou art, and unto dust shalt thou return*" (King James Version).

Everyman said, "Death, if I should take this pilgrimage and make my reckoning openly and fully and without failure, tell me, for the sake of Saint Charity, won't I come again to reside on Earth soon?"

"Saint Charity" is "holy charity."

Death said, "No, Everyman, if thou are once there at your destination in the afterlife, thou may never anymore come here to reside on Earth, trust me truly."

Everyman prayed:

"O gracious God, in the high seat celestial, have mercy on me in this most need!"

Everyman then asked Death:

"Shall I have no company of my acquaintance on this vale terrestrial — this earthly world — to guide me on that way?"

Death had said that Everyman can test his friends to see if any of them will accompany him, but Everyman was worried that no one would go with him.

Death said:

"Yes, you can have company — if any are so hardy and courageous that they would go with thee and bear thee company.

"But hurry so that thou will be going to God's magnificence so thou can give thy reckoning before His presence.

"What! Did thou think that thy life was *given* to thee, and thy worldly goods were also *given* to thee?"

"I had supposed so, truly," Everyman said.

Death said:

"No, no; thy life was only lent to thee. For, as soon as thou are dead and gone, another shall have it for a while and then go from life, just as thou have done.

"Everyman, thou are mad: foolish. Thou have thy five wits, and here on earth thou would not amend thy life. For I — Death — do come suddenly."

The five wits are memory, fantasy, judgment (aka estimation), imagination, and common sense.

Everyman had the knowledge that Death would come for him, yet he did not live his life better, and so now he was not prepared to appear before God.

Every illness that we endure during life is a reminder that Death will come for us one day.

Everyman said to himself:

"O wretched caitiff, where shall I flee so that I might escape this endless sorrow?"

Everyman then said:

"Now, gentle Death, spare me until tomorrow, so that I may amend myself with good reflection."

Death said:

"No, I will not consent to that, nor will I give respite to any man, but suddenly I shall smite each man to the heart without any reflection.

"And now I will go away out of thy sight.

"See that thou are ready quickly, for thou may say that this is the day that no living man may escape."

Death exited, leaving Everyman behind to test his friends and see if any of them would be willing to accompany him on his journey to see God.

Everyman said:

"Alas! I may well weep with sighs deep.

"Now I have no manner of company to help me in my journey, and to guard me, and also my written account of my life is completely unready.

"What shall I do now in order to excuse and defend me? I wish to God that I had never been born. If I had never been born, it would have been a very great profit to my soul, for now I fear huge and great pains.

"The time passes."

Everyman prayed:

"Lord, Who created everything, help!"

He then said:

"For although I mourn, it helps not at all.

"The day passes and is almost gone. I don't know well what I ought to do.

"To whom would I best make my anguish known?

"What if I spoke thereof to Fellowship, and told him about this sudden misfortune: my death! For in him is all my trust and faith. We have in the world been good friends in sport and play so many days."

Everyman saw Fellowship and said:

"I see him yonder certainly.

"I trust that he will bear me company, so therefore to him I will speak to ease my sorrow."

15

CHAPTER 2

Summary: Everyman tries to get his friends, family, and goods (wealth) to accompany him on his journey to have his life judged by God.

Fellowship entered the scene.

"We are well met, good Fellowship, and good morning," Everyman said.

Fellowship said:

"Everyman, good morning, by this day."

"By this day" is an oath.

Fellowship continued:

"Sir, why do thou look so pitiful and wretched? If anything is amiss, please tell me so that I may help to remedy the problem."

"Yes, good Fellowship, yes," Everyman said, "I am in great jeopardy."

"My true friend, tell me what is on your mind," Fellowship said. "I will not forsake thee to my life's end. We have been and will continue to be good company."

"That was well and lovingly spoken," Everyman said.

"Sir, I must know the reason for your sorrow," Fellowship said. "I feel pity to see you in any distress. If anyone has wronged you, you shall be revenged, even though I should be slain for thee on the ground, and even though I know beforehand that I should die."

"Truly, Fellowship, I give you great thanks," Everyman said.

"Tush!" Fellowship said. "I don't need your thanks. Tell me why you grieve, and say no more."

Everyman said, "If I should reveal my heart to you, and then you were to turn your mind away from me and would not comfort me when you hear me speaking, then I would be ten times sorrier and more grieved."

"Sir, I say in words what I will do in deed," Fellowship said.

"Then you are a good friend in times of need," Everyman said. "I have found you true before this time."

"And so you shall find me forevermore," Fellowship said, "for in faith, even if thou go to Hell, I will not forsake thee by the way."

"You speak like a good friend, and I believe you well," Everyman said. "I shall repay it, if I can."

Fellowship said:

"I speak of no deserving, by this day: For he who will say something and do nothing is not worthy to go with good company.

"Therefore, show me the grief of your mind, as to your most loving and kind friend."

Everyman said:

"I shall tell you how it is: I am commanded to go on a journey, a long way, hard and dangerous, and I am commanded to give a rigorous account of my life without delay before the High Judge Adonai."

"Adonai" is "God," aka "Lord."

Everyman continued:

"Therefore, I ask you to please bear me company, as you have promised to do, in this journey."

Fellowship said:

"This is a serious matter, indeed. A promise is a duty.

"But, if I should take such a voyage upon me, I know well that it would be to my pain. Also, it would certainly make me afraid."

In this society, a voyage is a long journey, not necessarily on water.

Fellowship continued:

"But let us deliberate here as well as we can, for your words would make a strong man afraid."

Everyman said, "Why, you said, if I had need, you would never forsake me, quick [alive] or dead, although it would mean for you to accompany me to Hell indeed."

"So I certainly said," Fellowship said. "But setting aside such pleasantries, truly, let me also ask: If we took such a journey, when should we return again?"

Pleasantries are pretty, polite words that don't mean much.

"Never again until the Day of Doom: Judgment Day," Everyman said.

In this society, "Doom" means "Judgment."

Fellowship said:

"Truly then, I will not come there.

"Who has brought to you these tidings?"

"Indeed, Death was here with me," Everyman said.

Fellowship said, "Now, by God Who has redeemed all of Humankind, if Death were the messenger, I will not go on that loathed journey for no man who is living today — not even for the father who begot me."

"You promised otherwise, by God," Everyman said.

"I know well what I said," Fellowship said. "I say so truly. And yet, if thou will eat and drink, and make good entertainment, or haunt the lusty company of women, I would not forsake you — while the day is clear. Trust me truly when I say that."

Fellowship is a clear-day friend: a fair-weather friend.

Everyman said, "Yes, you would be ready for those things. Your mind prefers to go to mirth, solace, and play than to bear me company in my long journey."

"Now, in good faith, I will not go that way," Fellowship said. "But, if thou will murder or kill any man, in that I will help thee with a good will."

Everyman said:

"Oh, that is foolish advice indeed."

It is not wise to murder someone, especially knowing that you will have to account for that murder before a just God.

Everyman then pleaded:

"Gentle, noble, gracious fellow, help me in my necessity: We have been friends for a long time, and now I need help. And now, gentle Fellowship, remember me in my need."

"Whether you have been friends with me or not, by Saint John, I will not go with thee," Fellowship said.

Saint John can be either John the Baptist or John the Evangelist.

"Yet, I ask thee to make the effort, and do so much for me as to accompany me, for Saint Charity, and comfort me until I come outside the town," Everyman said.

Fellowship replied:

"No. Even if thou would give me a new gown [an outer garment that men wore in the Middle Ages], I will not go a foot with thee. But, if thou had tarried here a while longer, I would not have left thee so.

"And now may God give thee success in thy journey! For from thee I will depart as fast as I may."

"Where are you going, Fellowship?" Everyman asked. "Will thou forsake me?"

"Yes, by my faith," Fellowship said. "To God I commend thee."

Everyman said, "Farewell, good Fellowship; because of thee, my heart is sore. Adieu forever, I shall see thee no more."

Fellowship said, "In faith, Everyman, farewell now at the end. Because of you, I will remember that parting is mourning."

Fellowship exited.

Everyman said to himself:

"Alas, shall Fellowship and I thus part truly?

"Ah, Our Lady, help!"

"Our Lady" is the Virgin Mary.

Everyman continued:

"Without any more comfort, see, Fellowship has forsaken me in my time of most need. For help in this world, where shall I turn?

"In the past, Fellowship here would make merry with me, and now he feels little sorrow for me.

"It is said, 'In prosperity men may find friends, who in adversity are completely unkind.'

"Now where shall I flee for help since Fellowship has forsaken me?

"To my kinsmen I will go truly, and I will plead with them to help me in my necessity.

"I believe that they will do so, for relatives will creep where they may not walk."

In other words, relatives will help you even in the most difficult circumstances. They will do what they can for you.

Everyman continued:

"I will talk to them and see if they will help me, for yonder I see them go."

Everyman's kindred and cousin entered the scene.

On stage, these are two people. In this society, a "cousin" can be a relative, but not necessarily a cousin as we define the term today. The word can also be used for a close friend. Readers should think of Kindred as representing Everyman's relatives, and of Cousin as representing Everyman's best friend or best friends. (Fellowship represents friends, but not best friends.)

"Where are you now, my friends and kinsmen?" Everyman asked.

Kindred said to Everyman:

"Here we are now at your service.

"Everyman, please tell us what you want in detail and don't leave anything out."

Cousin said, "Yes, Cousin Everyman, and to us declare if you are disposed to go anywhere, for, as you well know, we will live and die together."

Kindred said, "In wealth and woe — in good times and bad times — we will be with you, for with his kin a man may be bold."

In other words: A man can make difficult-to-fulfill requests of his relatives.

Everyman said:

"I give you great thanks, my kind friends and kinsmen.

"Now I shall show you the grief of my mind.

"I was given a command by a messenger — Death — who is a High King's — God's — chief officer.

"He ordered me to go on an unwelcome-to-me pilgrimage, and I know well I shall never come back again from that spiritual journey.

"Also, I must give a strict and accurate account of my life, for I have a great enemy who is lying in wait for me, who intends to hinder me."

The great enemy is Satan, who would love to take Everyman's soul and punish it in Hell.

"What account is that which you must render?" Kindred asked. "That is something I want to know."

Everyman answered:

"I must give an account of all my deeds. I must tell how I have lived and how I have spent my days.

"Also, I must tell about ill deeds that I have often done in my time since my life was lent to me, and I must tell about all the virtues that I have rejected and not practiced.

"Therefore, I plead with you to go there with me to help me to make my account of my life, for Saint Charity."

Cousin said, "What! To go there? Is that what you want? No, Everyman, I would prefer to fast on bread and water for five years or more."

"Alas, that I was ever born!" Everyman said. "For now I shall never be merry, if you forsake me."

Kindred said:

"Ah, sir! What! You are a merry man! You make jokes. Take good heart to you, cheer up, and make no moan or complaint.

"But one thing I warn you, by Saint Anne: As for me, you shall go alone."

Saint Anne is the mother of the Virgin Mary.

Everyman asked, "My cousin, won't you go with me?"

Cousin said. "No, by Our Lady, I have the cramp in my toe."

He had the gout, a disease that can be caused by rich food. His preferring to fast on bread and water for five years or more rather than accompany Everyman on his spiritual journey showed how much he did not want to go on that journey.

Cousin continued:

"Don't put your trust in me, for, God help me, I will deceive you in your most need."

Kindred said:

"You cannot entice us to go with you.

"You shall have my maid-servant with all my heart. She loves to go to feasts, there to be finely dressed and flirtatious, and to dance, and to gad about outside the house.

"I will give her permission to help you in that journey, if you and she may agree."

The maid-servant was unlikely to agree to go with Everyman.

Everyman said, "Now tell me the true intent of your mind. Will you go with me, or stay behind?"

"Stay behind!" Kindred said. "Yes, I will do that, if I can. Therefore, farewell until another day."

Kindred exited.

Everyman said:

"How should I be merry or glad? For men make fair promises to me, but when I have the most need, they forsake me.

"I am deceived, and that makes me sad."

Cousin said:

"Cousin Everyman, farewell now, for truly I will not go with you.

"Of my own life I also have to make a reckoning that I am not ready to make; therefore, I must tarry here."

Cousin will stay behind; if he is wise, he will spend the time amending his own life.

Cousin said:

"Now may God keep and protect thee, for now I go."

Cousin exited.

Everyman said to himself:

"Ah, Jesus, has it all come to this?

"Look, fair words make fools happy with a false sense of security.

"People make promises, but they will do nothing definite and real: They cannot be counted on."

Everyman continued:

"My kinsmen promised faithfully to steadfastly remain with me, and now they quickly flee away.

"Fellowship also promised to stay with me steadfastly.

"What friend would be best for me to find for myself?

"I waste my time staying here longer — yet in my mind I think of something.

"All my life I have loved Riches.

"If my Goods now might help me, it would make my heart very light.

"I will speak to Goods in this distress of mine.

"Where are thou, my Goods and Riches?"

From a corner, Goods spoke:

"Who is calling me? Everyman? What! Are you in a hurry? I lie here in corners bundled up and piled so high, and I am locked in chests so securely, and I am sacked in bags, as thou may see with thine eye, so that I cannot move. I lie in packs here on the ground!

"What do you want? Quickly tell me."

"Come here, Goods, in all the haste thou can make," Everyman said, "because I need your advice."

Goods came forward and said, "Sir, if you have sorrow or adversity in the world, I can help you to remedy that quickly."

Material problems can be solved with money.

Everyman said:

"It is another problem that grieves me, not a material one. My problem is not in this world. I tell thee that I am sent to go another way to give a comprehensive and rigorous account of my life before the highest Jupiter of all."

Jupiter is the mythological king of gods and men, but God is vastly superior to him.

Everyman continued:

"And all my life I have taken pleasure in thee, Goods.

"Therefore, I plead with thee now to go with me because, perhaps, before God Almighty thou may help to clean and purify my reckoning.

"For it is commonly said that money makes all right that is wrong: Money fixes all problems."

Goods replied:

"No, Everyman, I sing another song.

"I follow no man in such journeys, for, if I went with thee, thou would fare much the worse because of me.

"Why? Because thou did set thy mind on me.

"I have made thy reckoning blotted and illegible, with the result that thou cannot make out and clearly read truly thine account, and this happened because thou love me."

Matthew 6:24 states, "*No man can serve two masters: for either he will hate the one, and love the other; or else he will hold to the one, and despise the other. Ye cannot serve God and mammon*" (King James Version).

Everyman said:

"That would grieve me very much when I would appear before God to hear His verdict on my life.

"Get up! Let us go there together."

Everyman still wanted company beside him on his Day of Judgment.

Goods replied, "Nay, it must not be. I am too brittle, and I may not endure. I will follow no man one foot, you may be sure."

"Alas!" Everyman said. "I have loved thee, and I have had great pleasure all the days of my life on goods and treasure."

Goods said, "That is to thy damnation, I say without lies or falsehoods, for the love of me is contrary to the everlasting love, but if thou had loved me moderately during your life and had given part of me to the poor, then thou would not be in this distress, nor in this great trouble."

Everyman said, "Look, now I know I was deceived, before I was aware of my mistake, and I may blame it all on my waste of time."

Everyman was late in realizing that he should have been and should be charitable. He was late in realizing this because of the way he had spent his time.

"What! Do thou think that I belong to you?" Goods asked.

"I had supposed so," Everyman said.

Goods said:

"No, Everyman, I say that I do not belong to thee. Instead, for a while I was lent to thee; thou have had me in prosperity for a season.

"My nature is to kill man's soul. If I save one man, I ruin a thousand other men.

"Did thou think that I will follow thee?

"No, I will not follow thee as you pass from this world, truly."

"I had thought otherwise," Everyman said. "I had hoped that you would accompany me."

Goods said, "Therefore to thy soul Goods is a thief, for when thou are dead, my nature is to deceive another man in the same way that I have deceived thee, and all to his soul's shame and disgrace."

"O false Goods, may thou be cursed," Everyman said. "Thou traitor to God, thou have deceived me and caught me in thy snare."

Goods said, "By the Virgin Mary, thou brought thyself to this care and concern, and that is something of which I am very glad. I must laugh — I cannot be sad."

Don't blame wealth; blame yourself.

Everyman said:

"Ah, Goods, thou long have had my heartful love; I gave thee the love that I should have given to the Lord above.

"But won't thou go with me indeed? I ask thee to tell me the truth."

"No, I will not go with thee, so God help me," Goods said. "Therefore, farewell, and have a good day."

Goods exited.

Everyman said to himself:

"O, to whom shall I make my moan and request that they go with me in that heavy journey?

"First Fellowship said he would go with me. His words were very pleasant and gay, but afterward he left me alone.

"Then all in despair I spoke to my kinsmen, and also they gave me fair words, They lacked no pretty speeches, but they all forsook me in the end.

"Then I went to my Goods that I loved best, in hope to have found comfort, but there I had the least comfort because my Goods sharply told me that he brings many men into Hell.

"Then I was ashamed of myself, and so I am worthy to be blamed. Thus I may well hate myself.

"Whose advice shall I now take? I think that I shall never succeed until I go to my Good Deeds. But, alas! She is so weak that she can neither walk nor speak. Yet I will approach and ask her now."

CHAPTER 3

Summary: Everyman finds help. His Good Deeds will accompany him. Also, Knowledge helps Everyman to receive God's Grace.

"My Good Deeds, where are you?" Everyman asked.

Lying on the ground, Good Deeds spoke, "Here I lie cold on the ground. Thy sins have so sorely bound me that I cannot move."

"O Good Deeds, I stand in fear," Everyman said. "I must ask you for advice because help now would be very welcome."

Good Deeds replied:

"Everyman, I understand that you are summoned to account for your actions in life before the Messiah, King of Jerusalem.

"If you follow my advice, I will take that journey with you."

"That is why I have come to you to lament," Everyman said. "I plead with you to go with me."

Good Deeds said, "I would very much like to, but I truly cannot stand."

"Why, has anything happened to you?" Everyman asked.

Good Deeds replied:

"Yes, sir, and I may thank you for all of it.

"If you had perfectly cheered me by doing good deeds, your book of account would be completely ready for you to meet your Maker.

"Look also at the books of your works and deeds! See how they lie under the feet of your soul's heaviness and grief."

Pages from the books lay on the ground where they could be stepped on.

One book was an account of Everyman's deeds, and another was an account of Everyman's life.

Everyman tried to read the book of his deeds.

He said, "Our Lord Jesus help me, for I cannot see even one letter here in this book."

Good Deeds said, "There is a blind reckoning in times of distress!"

Everyman said, "Good Deeds, please help me in my need, or else I am forever damned indeed!

"Therefore, help me to make my reckoning before the Redeemer of all things, Who is King, and was King, and forever shall be King."

"Everyman, I am sorry about your fall, and I would eagerly help you, if I were able," Good Deeds said.

"Good Deeds, please give me your advice," Everyman said.

Good Deeds said:

"That I shall do truly, although I cannot walk on my feet.

"I have a sister called Knowledge who also shall go with you and shall remain with you to help you to make that dreadful reckoning of your deeds in life."

Knowledge is Awareness of One's Sins and How to Repent Them.

Knowledge entered the scene.

She said, "Everyman, I will go with thee and be thy guide. In thy greatest need, I will go by thy side."

Everyman said:

"I am now in good condition in everything, and I am wholly content with this good thing.

"Thanked be God my Creator."

Before Everyman would go to his Day of Judgment, Knowledge would take him to a priest to confess his sins.

Good Deeds said:

"And when he has brought you to the place where thou shall heal thee of thy pain, then you will go to your Judgment Day with your reckoning and Good Deeds together so they can make thee joyful at the heart before the blessed Trinity."

Earlier, Good Deeds had called Knowledge her sister, but just now she had called Knowledge "he." This may be a typo, but possibly gender does not apply to Knowledge, just as God the Creator is neither male nor female.

God is called Father, but the Bible includes maternal images of God:

Isaiah 42:14 states, "*I have long time holden my peace; I have been still, and refrained myself: now will I cry like a travailing woman; I will destroy and devour at once*" (King James Version).

Isaiah 66:13 states, "*As one whom his mother comforteth, so will I comfort you; and ye shall be comforted in Jerusalem*" (King James Version).

Good deeds are important, but in Christian theology, they are not enough to enter Heaven. That requires the grace — the gift — of God. One can get grace by sincerely repenting — and in Catholicism, by also confessing — one's sins.

In Catholicism, one must:

1) Repent one's sins and sincerely regret having committed them.

2) Confess one's sins.

3) Perform an act of penance, such as saying a set number of prayers.

People who sincerely repent their sins but die before they can confess them and perform an act of penance can climb the Mountain of Purgatory and go to Paradise.

Everyman said, "My Good Deeds, I give you great thanks. I am very happy certainly with your sweet words."

Knowledge said, "Now we go together lovingly to Confession, that cleansing river."

Everyman said:

"I weep because of joy. I wish that we were there.

"But please tell me where that holy man Confession dwells."

Knowledge answered:

"In the house of salvation: the church. We shall find him in that place where he shall comfort us by God's grace."

Confession entered the scene, and Knowledge took Everyman to Confession.

Knowledge said to Everyman:

"Look, this is Confession. Kneel down, and ask for mercy, for he is in good favor with God Almighty."

Everyman said to Confession:

"O glorious fountain that purifies all uncleanness, wash from me the unclean spots of vice, so that on me no sin may be seen. I come with Knowledge for my redemption and salvation.

"I want to be redeemed with heartful and full contrition and penitence, for I am commanded to undertake a pilgrimage and to make full accounts of my life and deeds before God.

"Now I ask you, Shrift [another name for Confession], mother of salvation, help my Good Deeds to stand and talk in response to my deserving-of-pity exclamation."

Of course, Everyman wanted Good Deeds to be able to walk and speak so that she could plead for him before God.

Confession said:

"I know your sorrow well, Everyman.

"Because you come to me with Knowledge, I will comfort you as well as I can; and I will give thee a precious jewel called *penance*, the expeller of adversity. With penance, your body shall be chastised with abstinence and with perseverance in God's service."

Penance consists of acts of self-punishment that show regret for having committed sin.

Confession continued:

"Here you shall receive this scourge — this whip — from me, which is a strong penance that you must endure."

Confession showed Everyman the scourge.

Confession continued:

"Remember thy Savior was scourged — whipped — for thee with painful lashes, and He endured it patiently: So must thou, before thou escape that painful pilgrimage: the one to Hell."

Confession then said:

"Knowledge, protect Everyman in this voyage — this pilgrimage, and by that time Good Deeds will be with thee."

Confession gave the scourge to Knowledge.

Confession then said to Everyman:

"But in any case, be a seeker of mercy, for your time draws near quickly. If you wish to be saved, ask God for mercy, and He will grant it truly.

"When Humankind commit themselves to the scourge of penitence, then Humankind shall find the oil of forgiveness."

Everyman said, "Thanked be God for His gracious work, for now I will begin my penance. This scourge has rejoiced and lightened my heart, although the knots of the whip are painful and hard.

Knowledge said, "Everyman, see to it that you fulfill your penance, despite whatever pain it causes you, and Knowledge shall give you advice whenever you want it about how you shall make your account clearly and readily and with all sins repented."

Everyman said:

"O eternal God, O heavenly figure, O way of righteousness, O goodly vision, Who descended down to Earth in a pure virgin, because He would redeem Everyman, whom Adam caused to be banned from the Garden of Eden by his disobedience.

"O blessed Godhead, exalted and high Divine, forgive me my grievous offence. Here I cry out and ask thee for mercy in the presence of Knowledge and Confession!

"O Spiritual Treasure, O Ransomer and Redeemer! Of all the world Hope and Conductor and Guide, Mirror of Joy, Founder of Mercy, Who illuminates Heaven and Earth thereby!

"Hear my urgent lamentation, although it is late in coming. Receive my unworthy prayers in this heavy-with-sin life of mine; although I am a sinner most abominable, yet let my name be written in Moses' tablets."

Some people thought that the two tablets of the Ten Commandments were symbols of Baptism and of Penance.

Everyman would have been most likely baptized soon after birth, and so now he wanted to do penance and be saved.

Everyman continued:

"O Mary, pray to the Maker of all things to help me at my ending — my death — and save me from the power of my enemy, Satan, for Death assails me strongly.

"And, Our Lady, I crave thy prayer so that by its means and by the means of your Son's passion, I may be a partner — a partaker — of your Son's glory. I beg you to help save my soul.

"Knowledge, give me the scourge of penance; with it, my flesh shall pay off its debt of sin. I will now begin, if God will give me grace."

Knowledge gave the scourge to Everyman.

Knowledge said, "Everyman, may God give you time and space — time and opportunity! Thus I bequeath you into the hands of our Savior. Now you may make your reckoning sure."

Everyman said:

"In the name of all the Holy Trinity, my body shall be punished severely."

Everyman took off his fine outer garment.

He then said:

"Take this, body, for the sin of the flesh."

He whipped himself.

These days, we are much more likely to say a number of prayers as penance than to whip ourselves.

Everyman then said:

"Also, thou — my body — delighted to go finely dressed in fine gay, colorful clothing. And in the way of damnation thou — my body — did bring me.

"Therefore, suffer now strokes and punishing."

Everyman whipped himself.

He then said:

"Now in penance I will wade the water clear, to save myself from the sharp fire of Purgatory."

Purgatory is a place where unconfessed but repented sins can be purged in a finite amount of time. This prepares the soul to enter Paradise.

In Dante's *Purgatory*, Purgatory is a mountain with seven ledges. On each ledge, a particular sin is purged and penitents learn a virtue that is opposed to that sin:

Ledge 1: Sin — Pride; Virtue — Humility

Ledge 2: Sin — Envy; Virtue — Kindness and Love of Others

Ledge 3: Sin — Wrath; Virtue — Meekness and Patience

Ledge 4: Sin — Sloth; Virtue — Zeal and Diligence

Ledge 5: Sin — Avariciousness (and Wastefulness); Virtue — Charity and Detachment from Riches and from What Riches can Buy

Avariciousness is greed: It can be greed for money or for what money can buy.

Ledge 6: Sin — Gluttony; Virtue — Abstinence or Temperance

Ledge 7: Sin — Lust; Virtue — Chastity or Proper Sex

Good Deeds arose from the ground.

Good Deeds said, "I thank God, now that I can walk and go, and now that I am delivered from my sickness and woe. Therefore, with Everyman I will go, and I will not spare anything I can do to help him. I will help him to declare his good works."

Knowledge said:

"Now, Everyman, be merry and glad. Your Good Deeds come now, so you may not be sad.

"Now is your Good Deeds whole and sound, going upright upon the ground."

Everyman said, "My heart is light, and shall be forevermore; Now will I whip myself faster than I did before."

Everyman scourged himself again.

Restored to health, Good Deeds said:

"Everyman pilgrim, my special friend, blessed be thou without end. The eternal glory is prepared for thee.

"You have me made whole and sound; therefore, I will stand by thee in every difficult trial."

Everyman said, "Welcome, my Good Deeds. Now I hear thy voice, I weep for very sweetness of love."

Knowledge said:

"Don't be sad anymore, but forever rejoice.

"In his throne above, God sees thy life. Put on this garment, which is wet with your tears, for thy benefit, or else before God you may miss it and wish that thou had it when you shall come to your journey's end."

Knowledge gave the garment to Everyman.

"Gentle Knowledge, what do you call this garment?" Everyman asked.

Knowledge answered:

"It is a garment of sorrow; it will rescue thee from everlasting pain.

"It is Contrition — regret for thy sins — that obtains forgiveness.

"It pleases God surpassingly well."

Good Deeds asked, "Everyman, will you wear it for your health: your salvation?"

Everyman put on the garment of sorrow: He regretted his sins.

Everyman said:

"Now blessed be Jesus, Mary's son, for now I have true contrition, and let us go now without tarrying here any longer.

"Good Deeds, have we purified our reckoning by washing away our sins?"

Good Deeds picked up the book of account and read it.

She said, "Yes, indeed, I have it here."

Everyman said, "Then I trust we need not fear. Now, friends, let us not separate."

"Everyman, we certainly will not part," Knowledge said.

Good Deeds said, "Yet thou must lead with thee three persons of great might."

She was calling on Everyman to be a leader and to bring with him three other pillars of strength.

"Who should they be?" Everyman asked.

Good Deeds said, "They are called Discretion and Strength, and thy Beauty may not stay behind."

Knowledge said, "Also, you must use your Five Wits as your counselors."

The Five Wits are memory, fantasy, judgment (aka estimation), imagination, and common sense.

"You must have them ready at all times," Good Deeds said.

"How shall I get them to come here?" Everyman asked.

"You must call them all together, and they will hear you immediately," Knowledge said.

Everyman said, "My friends — Discretion, Strength, Five Wits, and Beauty — come here, and be present."

CHAPTER 4

Summary: Everyman is joined by his personal attributes: Beauty, Discretion, Strength, and Five Wits. His personal attributes give him good advice, which he follows.

Beauty, Strength, Discretion, and Five Wits entered the scene.

Beauty said to Good Deeds, "Here at your will we are all ready. What do you want us to do?"

Good Deeds replied, "I want you to go with Everyman and help him in his pilgrimage. Consider this and decide: Will you go with him or not in that voyage?"

"All of us will bring him there, and we will be his help and comfort, you may believe me," Strength said.

"All together, we will go with him," Discretion said.

Everyman said:

"Almighty God, may Thou be loved!

"I give Thee praise because now that I have brought Strength, Discretion, Beauty, and Five Wits here, I lack nothing. And my Good Deeds, with Knowledge clear of sin and spotless, all are in my company at my will here.

"I desire no more for my business at hand."

"And I, Strength, will stand by you in distress, even though thou would in battle fight on the ground," Strength said.

Five Wits said, "And although your journey would be around the whole world, we will not depart either for sweet or for sour. We will not depart no matter what the circumstances may be: good or bad."

Beauty said, "I will not leave you until the hour of your death, whatsoever might happen."

Discretion said, "Everyman, consider this first of all. Go with good consideration, reflection, and deliberation. We all give you virtuous, beneficial notice that all shall be well."

Everyman said:

"My friends, listen to what I will tell you.

"I pray that God rewards you in His Heavenly sphere.

"Now listen all of you who are here, for I will make my testament here before all of you who are present: I will give away half my wealth in alms with both of my hands in the way of charity with good intent, and the other half I bequeath, to be returned where it ought to be."

Everyman wanted half his wealth to be used to repay all his debts so that he would owe nothing. The people who had loaned him money or who had sold him something on credit would be repaid what he owed them.

Everyman was not yet dead, and he could make a will and testament and do good deeds by leaving half his wealth to charity. This would strengthen Good Deeds, who would plead for him on the Day of Judgment.

Everyman continued:

"This I do in defiance of the fiend of hell, to entirely escape his peril, forever after this day."

Knowledge advised, "Everyman, listen to what I say: Go to the priest, I advise you, and receive from him in any case the holy sacrament and anointment together. Then shortly see that you return again to this place; we will all wait for you here."

Five Wits said:

"Yes, Everyman, hurry and make yourself ready for death. There is no emperor, king, duke, nor baron, who from God has a commission like the least, humblest, and lowliest priest in the world has. For of the blessed, pure, and benign sacraments, even the least, humblest, and lowliest priest in the world bears the keys and thereby has the cure needed to redeem Humankind.

"This cure is always sure, which God for our soul's medicine gave us out of His heart with great pain, here in this transitory life for thee and me.

"The blessed sacraments are seven in number:

"The first three are baptism, confirmation, and ordination to priesthood.

"The fourth is the sacrament of God's precious flesh and blood: the Eucharist.

"The fifth, sixth, and seventh are marriage, the holy extreme unction [Last Rites], and penance.

"These seven sacraments are good to remember; they are gracious sacraments of high divinity."

Everyman said, "Eagerly would I receive that holy body of the Eucharist, and I will go humbly and meekly to my spiritual father."

Five Wits said:

"Everyman, that is the best thing that you can do. God will bring you to salvation, for priesthood exceeds everything else.

"To all of us they teach holy scripture, and they convert Humankind from sin so Humankind can reach Heaven.

"God has given to priests more power than to any angel who is in Heaven.

"With five words a priest may consecrate God's body in flesh and blood, and he handles his Maker between his hands when he holds the consecrated bread and wine."

When a priest says, "*Hoc est enim corpus meum*" ("This is my very body") in a Mass, the bread of the Eucharist is converted into the body of Christ.

When a priest says, "*Hic est enim calix sanguinis mei*" ("This is the very cup of my blood") in a Mass, the wine of the Eucharist is converted into the blood of Christ.

Five Wits continued:

"The priest binds and unbinds all bands — shackles — both on Earth and in Heaven."

Matthew 16:19 states, "*And I will give unto thee the keys of the kingdom of heaven: and whatsoever thou shalt bind on earth shall be bound in heaven: and whatsoever thou shalt loose on earth shall be loosed in heaven*" (King James Version).

Five Wits continued:

"The priest administers all the seven sacraments.

"Though we kiss thy feet, thou are worthy of it.

"Thou, priest, are the surgeon who cures deadly sin.

"No remedy may we find under God, except all that come only from the priesthood.

"Everyman, God gave priests that dignity, and God sets them in His stead — as His representative — among us. Thus in degree and place they are above the angels."

Everyman went to the Priest to receive the last sacraments.

Knowledge said:

"If the priests are good, all you say is surely true.

"But when Jesus hanged on the cross with great pain, there He *gave* us out of his blessed heart the same sacraments in great torment. He — that omnipotent Lord — did not *sell* them to us.

"Therefore, Saint Peter the Apostle says that all they who buy or sell God their Savior or who take or count any money have Jesus' curse."

The sin of simony is the buying and selling of church offices and spiritual benefits for money. In Acts 8, Peter and John were using one of the gifts of God: the laying on of hands to convey the Holy Spirit. A man named Simon Magus was impressed by this and wanted to pay Peter and John money to teach him how to do that. Of course, Peter and John were insulted because the laying on of hands to convey the Holy Spirit is a free gift of God and is not for sale.

Knowledge continued:

"Sinful priests give the sinners bad examples. Their children sit by other men's fires, I have heard, and some bad priests haunt and frequent women's company, with unclean life, as lusts of lechery."

Catholic priests are not supposed to commit adultery and make men's wives pregnant, and Catholic priests are not supposed to have wives or to lead lustful lives.

Knowledge continued:

"These bad priests are made blind with sin."

Five Wits said:

"I trust to God that we may find no such bad priests.

"Therefore, let us honor priests and follow their doctrine for our soul's succor and assistance.

"We are their sheep, and they are shepherds by whom we all are kept in security, free from danger.

"Silence! For yonder I see Everyman coming here. He has made true satisfaction for his sins."

Everyman had atoned for his sins by sincerely repenting them and by receiving the necessary sacraments, including the Last Rites.

"I think that it is he, indeed," Good Deeds said.

Everyman returned, carrying a crucifix.

He said:

"Now may Jesus greatly help you!

"I have received the sacrament for my redemption [the Eucharist], and then I received my extreme unction [Last Rites]. Blessed be all they who counselled me to take it.

"And now, friends, let us go without longer delay.

"I thank God that you have waited so long for me.

"Now each of you set your hand on this cross, and quickly follow me. I go before, I lead, and there is where I would be.

"May God be our guide."

All of them grasped the crucifix in turn.

"Everyman, we will not go away from you, until you have finished this long journey," Strength said.

"I, Discretion, will stay by you also," Discretion said.

"And although this pilgrimage may be never so strong, I will never part from you," Knowledge said. "Everyman, I will be as loyal to thee as ever I was to Judas Maccabee."

The Maccabees organized and led the revolt against the Seleucid ruler Antiochus IV Epiphanes. They also reconsecrated the defiled Temple of Jerusalem.

The Maccabees had important victories, but in 160 B.C.E., Judas [sometimes called Judah] Maccabee died in the battle of Elasa.

Hanukkah, aka Chanukah, celebrates the recovery of Jerusalem and the rededication of the Second Temple, both of which were accomplished at the beginning of the Maccabean Revolt.

CHAPTER 5

Summary: Now that he has made his account book ready, Everyman goes close to his grave, accompanied by Strength, Discretion, Beauty, and Five Wits, and by Knowledge and Good Deeds. Strength, Discretion, Beauty, and Five Wits leave him, but Knowledge and Good Deeds go all the way to Everyman's grave. Everyman then dies and goes to meet God. He is accompanied only by Good Deeds. An Angel appears and speaks to Knowledge.

Accompanied by Strength, Discretion, Beauty, and Five Wits, by Knowledge, and by Good Deeds, Everyman went close to his grave.

He said:

"Alas! I am so faint that I may not stand; my limbs fold under me.

"Friends, let us not return to this land for all the world's gold, for into this cave — this grave — I must creep, and return to the earth, and to sleep there."

"What! Into this grave? Alas!" Beauty said.

"Yes, there you shall decay more and less — entirely," Everyman said.

"And what, should I smother here?" Beauty asked.

"Yes, by my faith, and you shall never more appear," Everyman said. "In this world we shall live no more, but in Heaven we shall live in the presence of the highest Lord of all."

"I cross out and cancel all this," Beauty said. "Adieu, by Saint John. I take my tap in my lap — that is, I will pack up — and I will be gone."

Beauty had promised to accompany Everyman only until the hour of his death. This was that hour. But Everyman had hoped that Beauty would continue to remain with him.

"What, Beauty?" Everyman asked. "To where will you go?"

"Silence!" Beauty said. "I am deaf to anything you say. I won't look behind me, not even if thou would give me all the gold in thy chest."

Beauty exited.

Everyman said:

"Alas! To what and whom may I trust?

"Beauty goes quickly away from me.

"She promised to live and die with me."

Strength said, "Everyman, I will also forsake and deny thee. I don't like thy undertaking at all."

Everyman said:

"Why, will all of you forsake me?

"Strength, wait a little space of time."

Strength said, "No, sir, by the rood — the cross — of grace, I will hurry away from thee quickly, even though thou weep to thy heart until it bursts."

Everyman said, "You would stay forever by me, you said."

Strength said, "Yes, I have conveyed and accompanied you far enough. You are old enough, I understand, to take on yourself your pilgrimage. I regret that I came here."

Everyman said, "Strength, I am to blame because you are displeased. Will you break your promise that is a debt that is owed to me?"

Strength said, "In faith, I don't care about breaking my oath. Thou are only a fool to complain. You expend your speech and waste your brain. Go, thrust thyself into the ground."

Strength exited.

Everyman said:

"I had thought for sure I would have found you dependable. He who trusts in his Strength is deceived in the end.

"Both Strength and Beauty have forsaken me, yet they made fair and loving promises to me."

Discretion said, "Everyman, I will follow Strength and be gone. As for me, I will leave you alone."

"Why, Discretion, will you forsake me?" Everyman asked.

Discretion answered, "Yes, indeed, I will go away from thee, for when Strength goes before, I follow after forevermore."

Everyman said, "Yet, I ask thee, for love of the Trinity, to look in my grave once out of pity."

Discretion said:

"No, so near to thy grave I will not come.

"Farewell, everyone."

Discretion followed Strength and exited.

Everyman said:

"O, all things fail us, except God alone.

Beauty, Strength, and Discretion have failed me, for when Death blows his blast, they all run away from me very fast."

The Five Wits said, "Everyman, I take my leave of thee now. I will follow the others, for here I forsake thee."

"Alas!" Everyman said. "Then I may wail and weep, for I took you for my best friend."

"I will no longer look after thee," the Five Wits said. "Now farewell, and there is an end."

The Five Wits exited.

"O, Jesus, help!" Everyman said. "All have forsaken me."

Good Deeds said, "No, Everyman, I will stay with thee. I will not forsake thee indeed. Thou shall find that I am a good friend in your need."

Everyman said:

"I give you great thanks, Good Deeds. Now I may see my true friends.

"They — the others — have forsaken me, every one of them. I loved them better than my good deeds alone.

"Knowledge, will you forsake me also?"

"Yes, Everyman, when you shall go to death," Knowledge said. "But for no manner of danger will I leave you before then."

Knowledge would stay until Everyman died, even if doing so would put Knowledge in danger.

Everyman said, "I give you great thanks, Knowledge, with all my heart."

Knowledge said, "I will not depart from here until I see where you shall go."

Knowledge would stay until Everyman died, and then Knowledge would stay longer until he learned where Everyman went: to Heaven or to Hell.

Everyman said:

"I think — alas! — that I must be gone to make my reckoning, and to pay my debts, for I see that my time on Earth is almost spent away.

"Use this as an example, all you who hear or see or read this, of how they whom I love best forsake me, except my Good Deeds, who remains with me like a true friend."

Good Deeds said:

"All earthly things are only vanity.

"Beauty, Strength, and Discretion do forsake Humankind, as do foolish friends and kinsmen, who spoke fair words."

Five Wits had also forsaken Humankind.

Good Deeds continued:

"All flee Humankind at his death except Good Deeds, and I am Good Deeds."

Knowledge was still present.

Everyman prayed, "Have mercy on me, God most mighty, and stand by me, thou mother and maiden: Mary."

A maiden is a virgin. The Virgin Mary gave birth to Jesus.

"Fear not, I will speak for thee," Good Deeds said.

"Here I cry, may God have mercy!" Everyman said.

Good Deeds prayed, "Shorten our end and diminish our pain. Let us go, and never come back again."

Everyman prayed:

"Into thy hands, Lord, I commit my soul with a prayer.

"Receive and accept it, Lord, so that it is not lost.

"As thou redeemed me, so defend me, and save me from the fiend's — Satan's — boast, so that I may appear with that blessed multitude of those who shall be saved at the Day of Doom: the Judgment Day.

"*In manus tuas*, most mighty One, forever *commendo spiritum meum*."

The Latin, which is from Luke 23:46 of the Vulgate Bible, states, "*Into thy hands I commend [commit] my spirit*."

The Vulgate Bible is a late-fourth-century Latin translation of the Bible. Saint Jerome did much of the translation.

Everyman and Good Deeds sank into the grave.

Knowledge said:

"Now that Everyman has suffered that which we all shall endure, Good Deeds shall make all safe, sure, and secure for him.

"Now that Everyman has made his ending, I think that I hear the angels sing and make great joy and melody, where Everyman's soul shall be received."

An Angel entered the scene and said to Knowledge:

"Come, excellent elect spouse to Jesus, here above thou shall go because of thy singular virtue."

The word "elect" means chosen by God for salvation.

In medieval theology, the soul was the spouse to Jesus. The soul is symbolically married to God.

The Angel continued speaking to Knowledge:

"Now that the soul is taken from the body, thy reckoning is crystal clear. Now thou shall go into the Heavenly sphere, the place where all of you who live well shall come after the Day of Doom [the Day of Judgment]."

Knowledge and the Angel exited.

Knowledge is Awareness of One's Sins and How to Repent Them. Knowledge is also symbolically married to God.

Knowledge has helped save many people, and Knowledge belongs in Paradise.

EPILOGUE

A Doctor of Theology entered the scene and said to you, the audience:

"This moral all men may have in mind:

"You hearers, old and young, take it as worth hearing.

"Forsake Pride, for Pride deceives you in the end.

"Remember: Beauty, Five Wits, Strength, and Discretion all at the last moment of life forsake every man.

A man's Good Deeds are the exception. These the dead man takes to Judgment Day.

"But beware, if a man's Good Deeds are small, the dead man has no help at all before God.

"No excuse may be made there on Judgment Day for any man.

"Alas, what shall the dead man do then? For after death no man may make amends because then mercy and pity forsake him.

"If his reckoning is not clear of sin, when he does come, God will say, *Ite, maledicti, in ignem eternum.*"

The Latin, which is from Matthew 25:41 of the Vulgate Bible, means, "*Go, accursed, into everlasting fire.*"

The Doctor of Theology continued:

"But he who has his account whole and sound shall be crowned high in Heaven.

"To that place may God bring us all, so that we may live body and soul together.

"The Trinity, help us to get there."

On Judgment Day, souls are reunited with their body.

The Doctor of Theology concluded:

"Amen, say you, for Saint Charity."

THUS ENDS THIS MORAL PLAY OF *EVERYMAN.*

NOTES

The Seven Deadly Sins, Part 1

This is an excerpt from my book *Dante's Purgatory: A Retelling in Prose*:

Dante and Virgil climbed the steps, and Virgil said to Dante, "Ask the angel now, humbly, to turn the keys and let us through the gate."

Dante knelt and begged the angel to let him and his companion through the gate.

First, the angel carved with his sword seven P's on Dante's forehead and told Dante, "Make sure that you heal these seven wounds as you journey up the mountain."

The angel thought, *The P is an abbreviation for* Peccatum, *the Latin word for "sin." All who journey up the mountain will heal seven wounds. Pride is the foundation of all sins; pride makes a person think that he or she is the center of the universe. These are the seven wounds, and these are illustrations of how these sinners think:*

1) Pride — A sinner who is guilty of Pride thinks, "I am the center of the universe, and I am better than other people. Quite simply, I am more important than other people."

2) Envy — A sinner who is guilty of Envy thinks, "I am the center of the universe, and if you have something I want, I envy you."

3) Wrath — A sinner who is guilty of Wrath thinks, "Because I am the center of the universe, everything ought to go my way, and when it does not, I get angry."

4) Sloth — A sinner who is guilty of Sloth thinks, "I am the center of the universe, so I don't have to work at something. Either other people can do my work for me, or they can give me credit for work I have not done because if I had done the work, I would have done it excellently."

5) Avariciousness and Prodigality — A sinner who is guilty of Avariciousness or Prodigality thinks, "I am the center of the universe, so I deserve to have what I want. If I want money, I get money and never spend it, or if I want the things that money can buy, then I spend every penny I can make or borrow to get what I want. Either way, I deserve to have what I want."

6) Gluttony — A sinner who is guilty of Gluttony thinks, "I am the center of the universe, so I deserve these three extra pieces of pie every night. This is my reward for myself for being so fabulous."

7) Lust — A sinner who is guilty of Lust thinks, "I am the center of the universe, so my needs take precedence over the needs of everyone else. If I want to get laid, it's OK if I lie to get someone in the sack and never call that person afterward. My sexual pleasure is more important than the hurt of someone who realizes that he or she has been used."

As saved souls climb the mountain, they will purge each of these deadly sins. They will learn some examples of the sins and they will learn some examples of the virtues that are opposed to the sins [...].

The Seven Deadly Sins, Part 2

Many of the sinners in the Inferno believe themselves to be the center of the universe. According to Dante's cosmology, the Earth is the center of the universe. Circle #9 of the inferno is at the center of the Earth. Lucifer is at the center of the Circle 9.

What is at the exact center of the universe? I know. It is inside Lucifer. The exact center of the universe is that place where food is not food anymore.

Five Wits

Here is some information from Wikipedia:

*In the time of William Shakespeare, there were commonly reckoned to be five wits and five senses. The five wits were sometimes taken to be synonymous with the five senses, but were otherwise also known and regarded as the **five inward wits**, distinguishing them from the five senses, which were the five outward wits.*

Much of this conflation has resulted from changes in meaning. In Early Modern English, "wit" and "sense" overlapped in meaning. Both could mean a faculty of perception (although this sense dropped from the word "wit" during the 17th century). Thus "five wits" and "five senses" could describe both groups of wits/senses, the inward and the outward, although the common distinction, where it was made, was "five wits" for the inward and "five senses" for the outward. [...]

The "inward" wits

Stephen Hawes' poem Graunde Amoure *shows that the five (inward) wits were "common wit", "imagination", "fantasy", "estimation", and "memory"."Common wit" corresponds to Aristotle's concept of* common sense (sensus communis), *and "estimation" roughly corresponds to the modern notion of instinct.*

Shakespeare himself refers to these wits several times, in Romeo and Juliet *(Act I, scene 4, and Act II, scene iv),* King Lear *(Act III, scene iv),* Much Ado About Nothing *(Act I, scene i, 55), and* Twelfth Night *(Act IV, scene ii, 92). He distinguished between the five wits and the five senses, as can be seen from Sonnet 141.*

The five wits are derived from the faculties of the soul that Aristotle describes in De Anima.

The inward wits are part of medieval psychological thought. Geoffrey Chaucer translated Boethius' Consolation of Philosophy *into Middle English. According to Chaucer's translation, "ymaginacioun" is the most basic internal faculty of perception. One can, with the imagination, call to mind the image of an object, either one directly experienced or a purely imaginary fabrication. Above that comes "resoun", by which such images of individual objects are related to the universal classes to which they belong. Above that comes "intelligence", which relates the universal classes to eternal "symple forme" (akin to a Platonic ideal). Humans are thus "sensible", "ymaginable", and "reasonable" (i.e. capable of sensing, imagination, and reason, as defined), all three of which feed into memory. (Intelligence is the sole remit of Divine Providence.)*

To that quartet is also added "phantasia", a creative facet of imagination. A famous example of this is given by Augustine, who distinguishes between imagining Carthage, from memory (since he had been there), and imagining Alexandria, a pure fantasy image of a place that he had never been to.

Source of Above: "Five wits." Wikipedia. Accessed 26 January 2023
https://en.wikipedia.org/wiki/Five_wits
NOTE: Possibly, "estimation" is "judgment" rather than "instinct."

Seven Sacraments

For Your Information:

The 7 Sacraments celebrated in the Catholic Church are Baptism, Confirmation, Eucharist, Penance and Reconciliation, Anointing of the Sick, Holy Orders, and Matrimony. They are divided into three categories: Sacrament of Initiation, Sacraments of Healing, and Sacraments at the Service of Communion.

Source of Above:

Allie Johnston, "The 7 Sacraments of the Catholic Church." Sadlier Religion Blog. 2 May 2021

https://www.sadlier.com/religion/blog/the-7-sacraments-of-the-catholic-church

Simony

Simony is the selling or buying of church offices or spiritual benefits.

For example, if I want to be the Bishop of a city, I could go to a corrupt Pope in the Middle Ages and pay money to become Bishop. This was a major problem and led to reform in the church, although periodic reform was occasionally needed in Dante's day, as well as in other times.

Sinners could also buy indulgences. The belief was that by paying money, the sinner would not be punished for certain sins. It is buying forgiveness of sin with money.

We read about Simon Magus in Acts 8. Peter and John are using one of the gifts of God: the laying on of hands to convey the Holy Spirit. Simon Magus is impressed by this and wants to pay Peter and John money to teach him how to do that. Of course, Peter and John are insulted because the laying on of hands to convey the Holy Spirit is a free gift of God and is not for sale (Acts 8.20-23; King James Version):

20: But Peter said unto him, Thy money perish with thee, because thou hast thought that the gift of God may be purchased with money.

21: Thou hast neither part nor lot in this matter: for thy heart is not right in the sight of God.

22: Repent therefore of this thy wickedness, and pray God, if perhaps the thought of thine heart may be forgiven thee.

23: For I perceive that thou art in the gall of bitterness, and in the bond of iniquity.

The apocryphal Acts of Peter tells us about Simon Magus' death. Simon became a magician, and he learned to fly. Saint Peter prays for Simon to fall out of the sky, and he does fall. (By the way, *magus* means "magician," and *apocryphal* means "of questionable or doubtful authenticity or authorship.")

In the third bolgia of Circle 8 in Dante's *Inferno*, the Simonists (who buy or sell church offices or spiritual benefits for money), including several popes, are punished. The Simonists are upside down in holes resembling baptismal fonts, and flames dance on their feet. Several things are going on here. First, the sinners are upside down because they placed things upside down in the living world — they placed material things before spiritual things, thus upsetting their proper order. Second, when Dante speaks with Pope Nicholas III, he is like a confessor by the side of an assassin who is soon to be buried alive upside down — Nicholas III will be pushed deeper into the hole when Pope Boniface VIII arrives in a few years. Third, we see a parody of Pentecost, when flames danced on the heads of the followers of Jesus. Finally, we see a parody of baptism, when water should be splashed on the head of the person being baptized. One thing to note in Canto 19 is that Dante the Pilgrim is in full agreement with Dante the Poet that these sinners richly deserve their punishment.

(Dante the Pilgrim is the Dante in the *Divine Comedy*; he is naïve and is still learning things. Dante the Poet is the older Dante who has experienced everything that Dante the Pilgrim is still experiencing in the *Divine Comedy*.)

Hannukah, aka Chanukah

For Your Information:

The miracle of the one-day supply of oil miraculously lasting eight days is described in the Talmud, committed to writing about 600 years after the events described in the books of Maccabees. The Talmud says that after the forces of Antiochus IV had been driven from the Temple, the Maccabees discovered that almost all of the ritual olive oil had been profaned. They found only a single container that was still sealed by the High Priest, with enough oil to keep the menorah in the Temple lit for a single day. They used this, yet it burned for eight days (the time it took to have new oil pressed and made ready).

Source: "Hannukah." Wikipedia. Accessed 26 January 2023 https://en.wikipedia.org/wiki/Hanukkah

Heaven and Hell

People going to Heaven drink from two streams.

One stream is called Lethe, which means "oblivion." Drinking from the water of the Lethe has the power to erase the memory of sin's sting when its water is drunk. You may remember your sins, but you will know that they have been forgiven, and you will rejoice and be happy that they have been forgiven. Gone will be the pain of the knowledge that you have sinned.

The other stream is called "Eunoë," which means "well minded" or "good memory," and it also has a special power. Drinking from the water of the Eunoë will restore the knowledge of every good deed that you have ever done.

We can imagine that in Hell one forgets every good deed that one has done, and that in Hell one remembers in great detail every bad deed that one has committed and the harm that resulted from it.

PETER SINGER: THE ARGUMENT TO ASSIST

• What are "absolute poverty" and "absolute affluence"?

Absolute poverty is when you can't provide yourself and your dependents with the necessities of life: food, shelter, and clothing. Many people in third-world nations suffer from absolute poverty.

Absolute affluence is when you have a significant amount of income above what is needed to provide yourself and your dependents with the necessities of life. Many people in Europe, North America, and Asia have absolute affluence.

Part of Singer's point is that people in first-world nations don't do enough to help people in third-world nations. This comes out in his discussion of the percentage of GNP [Gross National Product] that first-world nations spend on developmental assistance to third-world nations.

• What causes absolute poverty?

Singer believes that the World produces enough food to feed its population. (The Vatican agrees with this.) One problem is that we feed grain to cattle and other animals. This is an inefficient use of protein and food, as it takes a lot of pounds of grain to produce one pound of animal protein. If we were to become vegetarians, this would make a lot of grain available for purposes other than feeding cattle.

In general, Singer believes that the problem is one of distribution, not of production. The world produces enough food, but it isn't distributed to those who need it.

In addition, there may be economic exploitation of third-world countries by first-world countries.

• Is it a consequence of my spending money on a luxury item that someone in the third world dies?

According to Singer and consequentialism, yes. If you don't buy the luxury item and instead use the money to feed a starving person and save his life, then you have done a good thing. But if you do buy a luxury item and don't use the money to save the life of a person in a third-world nation, then you have done a bad thing. What you do with your money is up to you, but you are responsible for the consequences of your actions.

• **What is the "non-consequentialist view of responsibility"? (A theory of rights with an appended distinction between acts and omissions — killing and letting die.)**

According to a non-consequentialist view of responsibility, I can spend my money on a luxury item as long as my action does not leave the person in the third-world nation worse off than he was before. In other words, there is a distinction between killing and letting die. If I murder a person in a third-world nation by shooting him with a gun, then I am responsible for that person's death, but if that person dies because I didn't give money to charity, then I am not responsible for that person's death.

• **Why does Singer think we ought to reject the "non-consequentialist view of responsibility"?**

Singer thinks that it is an individual theory, based on people living separately in a state of nature. However, Singer knows that we are social creatures and that many of our accomplishments have come about because we are social creatures.

• **Explain how Singer arrives at the conclusion that "We ought to prevent some absolute poverty." What "plausible principle" does he use to get his argument started?**

Singer uses an analogy. On his walk to work is an ornamental pond. Suppose he were to see a child drowning in the pool. Shouldn't he rescue the child even if it is inconvenient to him? For example, even if he has to get his pants dirty and be late for a lecture, wouldn't we think that he ought to rescue the child? Of course we do. Singer believes that this situation is analogous to helping a person in a third-world nation.

The plausible principle he arrives at is this: "If something is in our power to prevent something bad from happening, without thereby sacrificing anything of comparable moral significance, we ought to do it."

- **Singer says that this plausible principle will please consequentialists, but non-consequentialists should accept it, too. Who does he have in mind here and why should they accept it? Why is the "plausible principle" not open to many of the standard counterexamples to consequentialism?**

Non-consequentialists will be pleased with the theory because of the part in the middle: "If something is in our power to prevent something bad from happening, <u>without thereby sacrificing anything of comparable moral significance</u>, we ought to do it." As Kantians know, things other than consequences are important; for example, keeping promises, not lying, etc. This plausible principle does not require us to lie or break a promise if doing so will have a good consequence.

- **What would happen if we took Singer's argument seriously and began to live our lives by it?**

It would have a big impact on our lives. We would give much, much more money to charity. Instead of having a second car or a second home, we would give the money to charity (if you think that saving someone's life is more important than having a second car or a second home).

- **Can we escape our obligation to help by saying that we ought to take care of our own first?**

We will not let our own family fall into absolute poverty while we help others. To do so would mean sacrificing something of comparable moral significance. However, we need to recognize that other people need help and that absolute poverty mainly exists in the poor nations.

- **Can we escape our obligation to help by appealing to property rights?**

Singer thinks that the theory of property rights leaves too much to chance. For example, you may be rich or poor because of chance. If you are born into a wealthy family, you will be rich. If you are born into a poor family, you will be poor. If you didn't know which family you would be born into ahead of time, wouldn't you hope that the rich would share with the poor?

• What is triage, and what is the argument that tries to show that we ought to adopt it as a policy toward the poor countries?

Triage is a way of dealing with the wounded in wartime and emergencies when medical resources are limited. The wounded are divided into three groups: 1) those who will probably get better without medical assistance, 2) those who will probably get better with medical assistance, and 3) those who will probably not get better with medical assistance, Because medical resources are limited, the idea is to make the best use of them by focusing on people in the middle group. That way, the greatest number of people will live.

People who make use of this argument believe that the world is like a lifeboat. If too many get on the lifeboat, it will sink and everyone will die. Therefore, we should focus on helping only those we think it possible to save without thereby jeopardizing ourselves. In this way of reasoning, people think that if we help the poorest of the poor, we will only be setting up conditions for even more people to die in the future. People will live to have lots of children, and the children will die.

• What is a "demographic transition"? What role does it play in Singer's argument against triage?

As countries become affluent, there is a demographic transition. Instead of having lots of children because so many die in infancy, people begin to have fewer children. Because of this, we need not be setting up conditions for even greater misery in the future. Singer does say, however, that we need to consider population growth in the kind of aid we give, and that we ought to give the kinds of aid that lead to the desired demographic transition.

• What kinds of aid ought we to give?

We ought to give the kinds of aid that will result in the desired demographic transition. Instead of simply giving away food, we might instead educate farmers about how to grow more plentiful crops or we might give away food-producing animals.

Notes:

The quotations by Peter Singer that appear in this essay are from his *Practical Ethics* (Cambridge, New York: Cambridge University Press, 1980).

A 20 January 2022 article titled "Extreme Poverty Has Been Sharply Cut. What Has Changed?" in *The New York Times* stated: "Bottom line: The U.N. goal was met. By 2015, the share of the world's population living in extreme poverty fell to 12 percent from 36 percent in 1990, a steep decline in just two and a half decades."

https://www.nytimes.com/2021/12/02/world/global-poverty-united-nations.html

Actions by governments and economic growth were responsible for most of the decline in extreme poverty.

BIBLE VERSES ABOUT GOOD DEEDS

(King James Version)

Proverbs 3:27-28 states:

27 Withhold not good from them to whom it is due, when it is in the power of thine hand to do it.

28 Say not unto thy neighbour, Go, and come again, and to morrow I will give; when thou hast it by thee.

Matthew 25:40 states:

40 And the King shall answer and say unto them, Verily I say unto you, Inasmuch as ye have done it unto one of the least of these my brethren, ye have done it unto me.

Galatians 6:9-10 states:

9 And let us not be weary in well doing: for in due season we shall reap, if we faint not.

10 As we have therefore opportunity, let us do good unto all men, especially unto them who are of the household of faith.

1 Timothy 6:17-18 states:

17 Charge them that are rich in this world, that they be not highminded, nor trust in uncertain riches, but in the living God, who giveth us richly all things to enjoy;

18 That they do good, that they be rich in good works, ready to distribute, willing to communicate;

Titus 3:8 states:

8 This is a faithful saying, and these things I will that thou affirm constantly, that they which have believed in God might be careful to maintain good works. These things are good and profitable unto men.

Hebrews 10:24 states:

24 And let us consider one another to provoke unto love and to good works:

Hebrews 13:16 states:

16 But to do good and to communicate forget not: for with such sacrifices God is well pleased.

James 2:14-17 states:

14 What doth it profit, my brethren, though a man say he hath faith, and have not works? can faith save him?

15 If a brother or sister be naked, and destitute of daily food,

16 And one of you say unto them, Depart in peace, be ye warmed and filled; notwithstanding ye give them not those things which are needful to the body; what doth it profit?

17 Even so faith, if it hath not works, is dead, being alone.

Matthew 5:16 states:

16 Let your light so shine before men, that they may see your good works, and glorify your Father which is in heaven.

Matthew 5:44 states:

44 But I say unto you, Love your enemies, bless them that curse you, do good to them that hate you, and pray for them which despitefully use you, and persecute you;

APPENDIX A: FAIR USE

§ 107. Limitations on exclusive rights: Fair use

Release date: 2004-04-30

Notwithstanding the provisions of sections 106 and 106A, the fair use of a copyrighted work, including such use by reproduction in copies or phonorecords or by any other means specified by that section, for purposes such as criticism, comment, news reporting, teaching (including multiple copies for classroom use), scholarship, or research, is not an infringement of copyright. In determining whether the use made of a work in any particular case is a fair use the factors to be considered shall include —

(1) the purpose and character of the use, including whether such use is of a commercial nature or is for nonprofit educational purposes;

(2) the nature of the copyrighted work;

(3) the amount and substantiality of the portion used in relation to the copyrighted work as a whole; and

(4) the effect of the use upon the potential market for or value of the copyrighted work.

The fact that a work is unpublished shall not itself bar a finding of fair use if such finding is made upon consideration of all the above factors.

Source of Fair Use information:

http://www.law.cornell.edu/uscode/17/107.html

APPENDIX B: ABOUT THE AUTHOR

It was a dark and stormy night. Suddenly a cry rang out, and on a hot summer night in 1954, Josephine, wife of Carl Bruce, gave birth to a boy — me. Unfortunately, this young married couple allowed Reuben Saturday, Josephine's brother, to name their first-born. Reuben, aka "The Joker," decided that Bruce was a nice name, so he decided to name me Bruce Bruce. I have gone by my middle name — David — ever since.

Being named Bruce David Bruce hasn't been all bad. Bank tellers remember me very quickly, so I don't often have to show an ID. It can be fun in charades, also. When I was a counselor as a teenager at Camp Echoing Hills in Warsaw, Ohio, a fellow counselor gave the signs for "sounds like" and "two words," then she pointed to a bruise on her leg twice. Bruise Bruise? Oh yeah, Bruce Bruce is the answer!

Uncle Reuben, by the way, gave me a haircut when I was in kindergarten. He cut my hair short and shaved a small bald spot on the back of my head. My mother wouldn't let me go to school until the bald spot grew out again.

Of all my brothers and sisters (six in all), I am the only transplant to Athens, Ohio. I was born in Newark, Ohio, and have lived all around Southeastern Ohio. However, I moved to Athens to go to Ohio University and have never left.

At Ohio U, I never could make up my mind whether to major in English or Philosophy, so I got a bachelor's degree with a double major in both areas, then I added a Master of Arts degree in English and a Master of Arts degree in Philosophy. Yes, I have my MAMA degree.

Currently, and for a long time to come (I eat fruits and veggies), I am spending my retirement writing books such as *Nadia Comaneci: Perfect 10*, *The Funniest People in Comedy*, *Homer's* Iliad: *A Retelling in Prose*, and *William Shakespeare's* Hamlet: *A Retelling in Prose.*

If all goes well, I will publish one or two books a year for the rest of my life. (On the other hand, a good way to make God laugh is to tell Her your plans.)

By the way, my sister Brenda Kennedy writes romances such as *A New Beginning* and *Shattered Dreams.*

APPENDIX C: SOME BOOKS BY DAVID BRUCE

Retellings of a Classic Work of Literature

Arden of Faversham*: A Retelling*

Ben Jonson's The Alchemist: *A Retelling*

Ben Jonson's The Arraignment, or Poetaster: *A Retelling*

Ben Jonson's Bartholomew Fair: *A Retelling*

Ben Jonson's The Case is Altered: *A Retelling*

Ben Jonson's Catiline's Conspiracy: *A Retelling*

Ben Jonson's The Devil is an Ass: *A Retelling*

Ben Jonson's Epicene: *A Retelling*

Ben Jonson's Every Man in His Humor: *A Retelling*

Ben Jonson's Every Man Out of His Humor: *A Retelling*

Ben Jonson's The Fountain of Self-Love, or Cynthia's Revels: *A Retelling*

Ben Jonson's The Magnetic Lady, or Humors Reconciled: *A Retelling*

Ben Jonson's The New Inn, or The Light Heart: *A Retelling*

Ben Jonson's Sejanus' Fall: *A Retelling*

Ben Jonson's The Staple of News: *A Retelling*

Ben Jonson's A Tale of a Tub: *A Retelling*

Ben Jonson's Volpone, or the Fox: *A Retelling*

Christopher Marlowe's Complete Plays: Retellings

Christopher Marlowe's Dido, Queen of Carthage: *A Retelling*

Christopher Marlowe's Doctor Faustus: *Retellings of the 1604 A-Text and of the 1616 B-Text*

Christopher Marlowe's Edward II: *A Retelling*

Christopher Marlowe's The Massacre at Paris: *A Retelling*

Christopher Marlowe's The Rich Jew of Malta: *A Retelling*

Christopher Marlowe's Tamburlaine, Parts 1 and 2: *Retellings*

Dante's Divine Comedy: *A Retelling in Prose*

Dante's Inferno: *A Retelling in Prose*

Dante's Purgatory: *A Retelling in Prose*

Dante's Paradise: *A Retelling in Prose*

The Famous Victories of Henry V: *A Retelling*

From the Iliad *to the* Odyssey: *A Retelling in Prose of Quintus of Smyrna's* Posthomerica

George Chapman, Ben Jonson, and John Marston's Eastward Ho! *A Retelling*

George Peele's The Arraignment of Paris: *A Retelling*

George Peele's The Battle of Alcazar: *A Retelling*

George's Peele's David and Bathsheba, and the Tragedy of Absalom: *A Retelling*

George Peele's Edward I: *A Retelling*

George Peele's The Old Wives' Tale: *A Retelling*

George-a-Greene: *A Retelling*

The History of King Leir: *A Retelling*

Homer's Iliad: *A Retelling in Prose*

Homer's Odyssey: *A Retelling in Prose*

J.W. Gent.'s The Valiant Scot: *A Retelling*

Jason and the Argonauts: A Retelling in Prose of Apollonius of Rhodes' Argonautica

John Ford: Eight Plays Translated into Modern English

John Ford's The Broken Heart: *A Retelling*

John Ford's The Fancies, Chaste and Noble: *A Retelling*

John Ford's The Lady's Trial: *A Retelling*

John Ford's The Lover's Melancholy: *A Retelling*

John Ford's Love's Sacrifice: *A Retelling*

John Ford's Perkin Warbeck: *A Retelling*

John Ford's The Queen: *A Retelling*

John Ford's 'Tis Pity She's a Whore: *A Retelling*

John Lyly's Campaspe: *A Retelling*

John Lyly's Endymion, The Man in the Moon: *A Retelling*

John Lyly's Galatea: *A Retelling*

John Lyly's Love's Metamorphosis: *A Retelling*

John Lyly's Midas: *A Retelling*

John Lyly's Mother Bombie: *A Retelling*

John Lyly's Sappho and Phao: *A Retelling*

John Lyly's The Woman in the Moon: *A Retelling*

John Webster's The White Devil: *A Retelling*

King Edward III: *A Retelling*

Mankind: *A Medieval Morality Play* (A Retelling)

Margaret Cavendish's The Unnatural Tragedy: *A Retelling*

The Merry Devil of Edmonton: *A Retelling*

The Summoning of Everyman: *A Medieval Morality Play* (A Retelling)

Robert Greene's Friar Bacon and Friar Bungay: *A Retelling*

The Taming of a Shrew: *A Retelling*

Tarlton's Jests: A Retelling

Thomas Middleton's A Chaste Maid in Cheapside: *A Retelling*

Thomas Middleton's Women Beware Women: *A Retelling*

Thomas Middleton and Thomas Dekker's The Roaring Girl: *A Retelling*
Thomas Middleton and William Rowley's The Changeling: *A Retelling*
The Trojan War and Its Aftermath: Four Ancient Epic Poems
Virgil's Aeneid: *A Retelling in Prose*
William Shakespeare's 5 Late Romances: Retellings in Prose
William Shakespeare's 10 Histories: Retellings in Prose
William Shakespeare's 11 Tragedies: Retellings in Prose
William Shakespeare's 12 Comedies: Retellings in Prose
William Shakespeare's 38 Plays: Retellings in Prose
William Shakespeare's 1 Henry IV, aka Henry IV, Part 1: A Retelling in Prose
William Shakespeare's 2 Henry IV, aka Henry IV, Part 2: A Retelling in Prose
William Shakespeare's 1 Henry VI, aka Henry VI, Part 1: A Retelling in Prose
William Shakespeare's 2 Henry VI, aka Henry VI, Part 2: A Retelling in Prose
William Shakespeare's 3 Henry VI, aka Henry VI, Part 3: A Retelling in Prose
William Shakespeare's All's Well that Ends Well: *A Retelling in Prose*
William Shakespeare's Antony and Cleopatra: *A Retelling in Prose*
William Shakespeare's As You Like It: *A Retelling in Prose*
William Shakespeare's The Comedy of Errors: *A Retelling in Prose*
William Shakespeare's Coriolanus: *A Retelling in Prose*
William Shakespeare's Cymbeline: *A Retelling in Prose*
William Shakespeare's Hamlet: *A Retelling in Prose*
William Shakespeare's Henry V: *A Retelling in Prose*
William Shakespeare's Henry VIII: *A Retelling in Prose*
William Shakespeare's Julius Caesar: *A Retelling in Prose*
William Shakespeare's King John: *A Retelling in Prose*
William Shakespeare's King Lear: *A Retelling in Prose*
William Shakespeare's Love's Labor's Lost: *A Retelling in Prose*
William Shakespeare's Macbeth: *A Retelling in Prose*
William Shakespeare's Measure for Measure: *A Retelling in Prose*
William Shakespeare's The Merchant of Venice: *A Retelling in Prose*
William Shakespeare's The Merry Wives of Windsor: *A Retelling in Prose*
William Shakespeare's A Midsummer Night's Dream: *A Retelling in Prose*
William Shakespeare's Much Ado About Nothing: *A Retelling in Prose*
William Shakespeare's Othello: *A Retelling in Prose*
William Shakespeare's Pericles, Prince of Tyre: *A Retelling in Prose*
William Shakespeare's Richard II: *A Retelling in Prose*
William Shakespeare's Richard III: *A Retelling in Prose*
William Shakespeare's Romeo and Juliet: *A Retelling in Prose*
William Shakespeare's The Taming of the Shrew: *A Retelling in Prose*

William Shakespeare's The Tempest: *A Retelling in Prose*
William Shakespeare's Timon of Athens: *A Retelling in Prose*
William Shakespeare's Titus Andronicus: *A Retelling in Prose*
William Shakespeare's Troilus and Cressida: *A Retelling in Prose*
William Shakespeare's Twelfth Night: *A Retelling in Prose*
William Shakespeare's The Two Gentlemen of Verona: *A Retelling in Prose*
William Shakespeare's The Two Noble Kinsmen: *A Retelling in Prose*
William Shakespeare's The Winter's Tale: *A Retelling in Prose*